My First Atlas

Nicholas Harris

Illustrations by
Gary Hincks and Nicki Palin

HINKLER
BOOKS

CONTENTS

THE WORLD

THE WORLD is round. So, to make a map of the world appear on a flat page, the world's curved surface must be flattened out and parts of it stretched. The world map *(below)* is the result. The maps in this atlas show different areas of the world. Look for the little world map printed on each page. The part shaded red shows where in the world that area is situated.

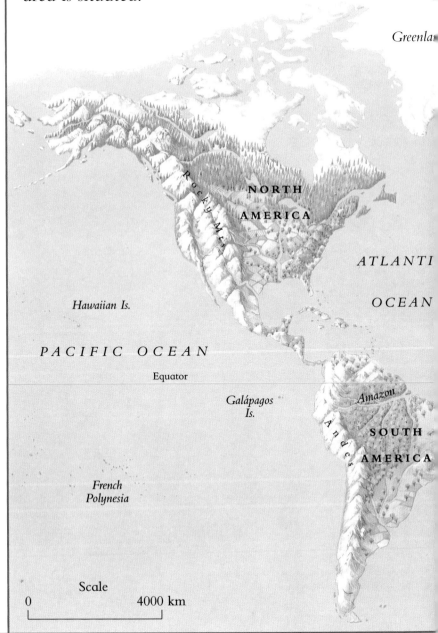

HOW TO USE THIS ATLAS

The maps in this atlas have been specially drawn to show where different kinds of landscape are found.

 Arctic lands (tundra)

 Forest and woodlands

 Grassland

 Mountains

 Coniferous forest

 Marshes

 Desert

 Farmland

 Rivers and lakes

A scale bar *(below)* tells us how far distances on the map are in the real world. You can use it to work out longer or shorter distances.

Scale

0   200 km

Boundaries between countries are shown in this atlas by red lines *(below left)*. Boundaries between states within countries, or disputed boundaries, are both shown by broken lines *(below right)*.

ARCTIC OCEAN

Svalbard

Iceland

Ural Mts.

Ob

EUROPE

Aleutian Is.

ASIA

Gobi

PACIFIC OCEAN

Himalayas

Hawaiian Is.

Sahara Desert

Nile

Marshall Is.

Kiribati

Seychelles

New Guinea

AFRICA

Solomon Is.

INDIAN

Samoa

Fiji

Tonga

OCEAN

AUSTRALIA

New Caledonia

New Zealand

Kergeulen Is.

Killer whales swim in the Arctic seas.

This pipeline carries oil across Alaska. It is built above the ground so that caribou can pass underneath it.

Ellesmere Island

DID YOU KNOW . . ?

Canada has two languages, English and French. The French were the first Europeans to settle Canada but the British won control after a war. French is still spoken in the province of Québec and English elsewhere.

ALASKA
(US)

■ ANCHORAGE

ARCTIC OCEAN

Banks Island

Victoria Island

Great Bear Lake

YUKON

Yukon

Mackenzie

PACIFIC OCEAN

NORTHWEST
TERRITORIES

NUNAVUT

Great Slave Lake

R o c k y   M o u n t a i n s

C A N A D A

BRITISH
COLUMBIA

ALBERTA

■ EDMONTON

MANITOBA

SASKATCHEWAN

Saskatchewan

■ VANCOUVER

■ CALGARY

■ REGINA

■ WINNIPEG

For many years, the native peoples of Canada's western coast carved totem poles. The poles stand at the doorways of their village homes. The wood carvings show figures and animals that were important in the history of their families.

CANADA AND THE ARCTIC

CANADA is the second largest country in the world, after Russia. The northern region of Canada, known as tundra, is a frozen wasteland for about nine months of the year. Further south lie vast coniferous forests. Rising in the west are the craggy Rocky and Coast Mountains. Nearly all Canada's cities lie close to the border with the USA and in the fertile grasslands known as the prairies. Alaska, a state of the USA, is a land of tundra and forests.

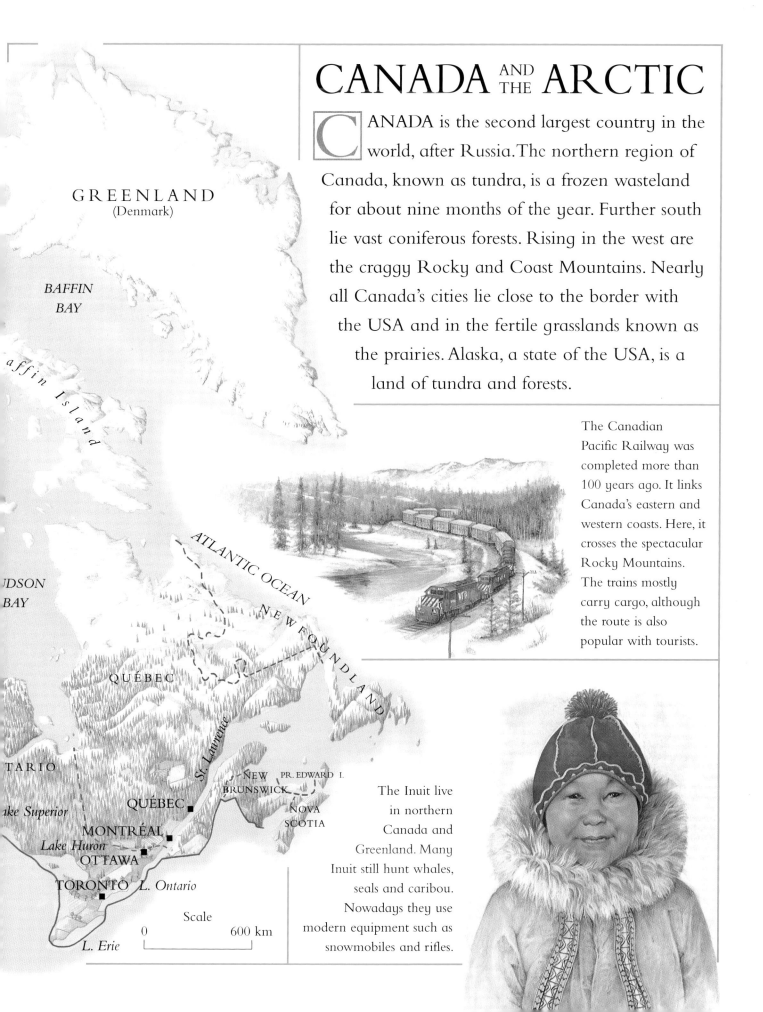

GREENLAND
(Denmark)

BAFFIN BAY

Baffin Island

HUDSON BAY

ATLANTIC OCEAN

NEWFOUNDLAND

QUÉBEC

St. Lawrence

ONTARIO

NEW BRUNSWICK

PR. EDWARD I.

NOVA SCOTIA

Lake Superior

QUÉBEC ■

MONTRÉAL ■

Lake Huron

OTTAWA ■

TORONTO ■ L. Ontario

L. Erie

Scale

0   600 km

The Canadian Pacific Railway was completed more than 100 years ago. It links Canada's eastern and western coasts. Here, it crosses the spectacular Rocky Mountains. The trains mostly carry cargo, although the route is also popular with tourists.

The Inuit live in northern Canada and Greenland. Many Inuit still hunt whales, seals and caribou. Nowadays they use modern equipment such as snowmobiles and rifles.

UNITED STATES OF AMERICA

THE United States of America stretches from the Atlantic to the Pacific coasts of North America. Eastern USA is made up of the wooded Appalachian Mountains and fertile plains. The centre of the country, the Mississippi lowlands, is mainly farmland. In the west, the landscape is mountainous. Here the climate, apart from on the Pacific coast, is much drier.

Once settled only by Native Americans, the USA is now home to people who came from all over the world to live there.

Scale
0   500 km

Baseball is a popular summer sport in the USA. It is played between two teams of nine players on a diamond-shaped pitch. Batters attempt to strike a ball thrown towards them by a pitcher.

The centres of many American cities are often crowded with skyscrapers. Seattle, in the northwest, also has the Space Needle. From the top there is a superb view of the city and the mountains nearby.

SEATTLE
WASHINGTON
MONTANA
OREGON
IDAHO
Snake
WYOMING
SALT LAKE CITY
NEVADA
DENVER
UTAH
SAN FRANCISCO
COLORA
CALIFORNIA
Colorado
LOS ANGELES
ARIZONA
NEW
MEXICO
PHOENIX
Rio
PACIFIC OCEAN

HONOLULU
HAWAII

DID YOU KNOW . . ?

California lies across a giant crack in the Earth's surface called the San Andreas Fault. Here there is an ever-present risk of a major earthquake. The last one destroyed San Francisco in 1906.

The Everglades are a large area of wetlands in southern Florida. Some people want to drain part of the land, a haven for rare animals such as alligators and wading birds, for farms.

NORTH DAKOTA

MINNESOTA

Lake Superior

MAINE

MINNEAPOLIS

WISCONSIN

MICHIGAN

Lake Huron

Lake Ontario

VT. N.H.

BOSTON

SOUTH DAKOTA

L. Michigan

NEW YORK

MASS.

CONN.

R.I.

CONN.	CONNECTICUT
N.H.	NEW HAMPSHIRE
MASS.	MASSACHUSETTS
MD.	MARYLAND
R.I.	RHODE ISLAND
VT.	VERMONT

IOWA

CHICAGO

DETROIT

L. Erie

NEW YORK

Missouri

NEBRASKA

INDIANA

OHIO

CLEVELAND

PHILADELPHIA

PENNSYLVANIA

NEW JERSEY

WASHINGTON

MD.

DELAWARE

ILLINOIS

Ohio

WEST VIRGINIA

KANSAS CITY

ST. LOUIS

VIRGINIA

KANSAS

MISSOURI

KENTUCKY

Appalachian Mts.

NORTH CAROLINA

Arkansas

TENNESSEE

OKLAHOMA

ARKANSAS

Mississippi

SOUTH CAROLINA

ATLANTIC OCEAN

ATLANTA

DALLAS

ALABAMA

GEORGIA

TEXAS

MISSISSIPPI

The Statue of Liberty stands on an island at the entrance to New York harbour. The copper statue was built as a gift of friendship from France to the USA.

LOUISIANA

NEW ORLEANS

FLORIDA

HOUSTON

MIAMI

GULF OF MEXICO

Cotton is an important crop in the south. It was once hand-picked by black slaves brought by force from Africa. Now modern machines do the job.

Much of northern Mexico is covered by desert. The cactus is often the only plant life there.

DID YOU KNOW . . ?

Mexico City, the capital of Mexico, lies at more than 2000 metres above sea level. With more than 20 million people, it is one of the largest cities in the world – and one of the most polluted.

MEXICALI

Scale

0   400 km

GULF OF CALIFORNIA

Sierra Madre

Río Grande

MONTERREY

M E X I C O

GULF OF MEXICO

GUADALAJARA

MÉRIDA

MEXICO CITY

PACIFIC OCEAN

BELIZE

GUATEMALA

EL SALVADOR

In many Central American and Caribbean countries, growing bananas is the most important industry. As the bananas grow, workers cover them with bags to protect them from insects. The bananas are cut down while they are still green. They ripen just before they go on sale.

The Panama Canal links the Atlantic and Pacific Oceans. Before the canal was built, ships had to go around the stormy seas off the southern tip of South America. A series of locks were built to take canal traffic across the 80-kilometre stretch of land. Small trains help pull the ships through the locks.

MEXICO AND CENTRAL AMERICA

MEXICO and the Central American countries stretch from the United States in the north to South America in the south. A mountain chain runs all the way down. There are many active volcanoes and the land is regularly shaken by earthquakes, too. In the north the climate is dry, but further south there is tropical rainforest.

The Caribbean islands have a hot, wet climate. They often suffer fierce hurricanes.

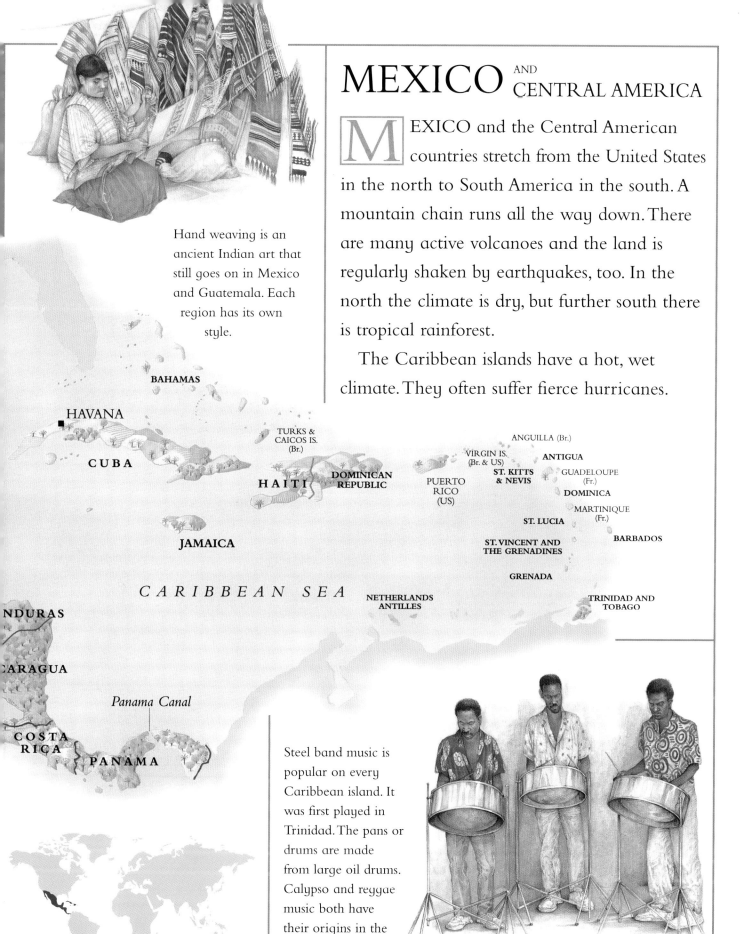

Hand weaving is an ancient Indian art that still goes on in Mexico and Guatemala. Each region has its own style.

BAHAMAS

HAVANA

CUBA

TURKS & CAICOS IS. (Br.)

HAITI

DOMINICAN REPUBLIC

JAMAICA

PUERTO RICO (US)

VIRGIN IS. (Br. & US)

ANGUILLA (Br.)

ANTIGUA

ST. KITTS & NEVIS

GUADELOUPE (Fr.)

DOMINICA

MARTINIQUE (Fr.)

ST. LUCIA

BARBADOS

ST. VINCENT AND THE GRENADINES

GRENADA

CARIBBEAN SEA

NETHERLANDS ANTILLES

TRINIDAD AND TOBAGO

NDURAS

ARAGUA

Panama Canal

COSTA RICA

PANAMA

Steel band music is popular on every Caribbean island. It was first played in Trinidad. The pans or drums are made from large oil drums. Calypso and reggae music both have their origins in the Caribbean.

SOUTH AMERICA

THE CLIMATE in the northern part of South America is hot and rainy. The great Amazon Rainforest fills the Amazon River basin, a vast lowland area lying between the Andes and the Brazilian Highlands. The Andes mountains stretch all the way down the western edge of the continent to its cold, stormy southern tip, Cape Horn. Most of South America's farmland and cities are in the east, in southeastern Brazil and northern Argentina.

These Indians take home their catch – an anaconda.

DID YOU KNOW . . ?

The Amazon River is 6500 km long. It carries more water than any other river – greater than that of the world's eight longest rivers put together.

RECIFE

Scale

0   600 km

B R A Z I L

Brazilian Highlands

Amazon Rainforest

SURINAME   FRENCH GUIANA

GUYANA

Amazon

VENEZUELA

Orinoco

Negro

Madeira

CARACAS

BOGOTÁ

COLOMBIA

BOLIVIA

LA PAZ

A n d e s

L. Titicaca

P E R U

LIMA

QUITO

ECUADOR

PACIFIC OCEAN

RIO DE JANEIRO

Mardi Gras, or Shrove Tuesday, is a time of carnival in Rio de Janeiro, Brazil. There are parties and balls. People dress up in amazing costumes and parade through the streets

These children live in a shantytown on the edge of one of South America's huge cities. There are not enough places for poorer people to live in the cities, so many build their own houses out of spare pieces of iron and wood.

SÃO PAULO

PARAGUAY

Paran...

URUGUAY

MONTEVIDEO

BUENOS AIRES

ARGENTINA

SANTIAGO

A n d e s

C H I L E

ATLANTIC OCEAN

Patagonia

Falkland Is. (Br.)

Tierra del Fuego

Cape Horn

A condor glides without flapping its wings for many kilometres over the barren and remote southern Andes mountains.

Indian peoples who live in the mountains of Peru and Bolivia still have their traditional dress and customs.

The Berbers come from Morocco. Each year, Berber girls dress in a special costume and go to a ceremony where they are chosen as brides.

The Wodaabe people of Niger live by herding cattle and sheep in the dry grasslands close to the Sahara Desert. The men wear special make-up for performing a courtship dance.

MEDITERRANEAN SEA

ATLANTIC OCEAN

ALGIERS
TUNIS
CASABLANCA
TUNISIA
MOROCCO
Atlas Mountains
ALGERIA
LI

WESTERN SAHARA

S a h a r a   D e

MAURITANIA

MALI

NIGER

DAKAR
SENEGAL
THE GAMBIA
GUINEA-BISSAU
GUINEA
SIERRA LEONE
LIBERIA
CÔTE D'IVOIRE
BURKINA FASO
Niger
GHANA
TOGO
BENIN
NIGERIA
LAGOS
ACCRA
CAMEROON
EQUATORIAL GUINEA

Lake Chad

GULF OF GUINEA

DID YOU KNOW . . ?

Most of the Sahara Desert is not sandy at all, but covered with rock and gravel. At night, it is usually freezing cold.

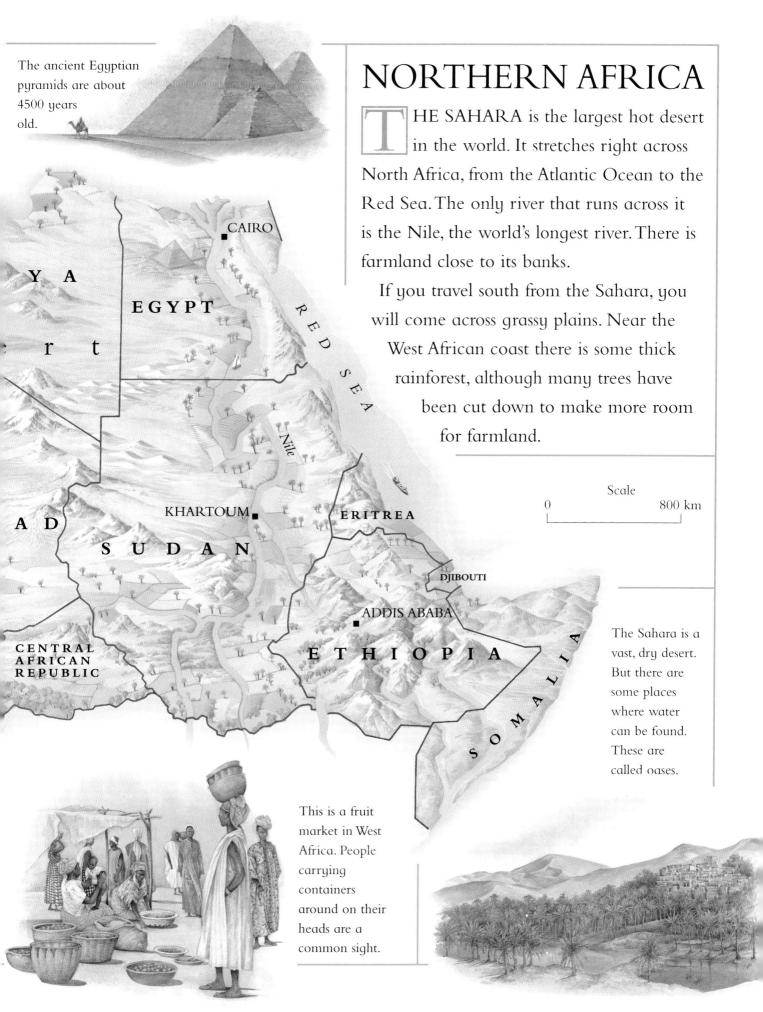

The ancient Egyptian pyramids are about 4500 years old.

NORTHERN AFRICA

THE SAHARA is the largest hot desert in the world. It stretches right across North Africa, from the Atlantic Ocean to the Red Sea. The only river that runs across it is the Nile, the world's longest river. There is farmland close to its banks.

If you travel south from the Sahara, you will come across grassy plains. Near the West African coast there is some thick rainforest, although many trees have been cut down to make more room for farmland.

Scale

0   800 km

CAIRO

YA

EGYPT

r t

RED SEA

Nile

KHARTOUM

ERITREA

AD

SUDAN

DJIBOUTI

ADDIS ABABA

CENTRAL
AFRICAN
REPUBLIC

ETHIOPIA

SOMALIA

The Sahara is a vast, dry desert. But there are some places where water can be found. These are called oases.

This is a fruit market in West Africa. People carrying containers around on their heads are a common sight.

Many Africans follow the traditional religions of their ancestors. Their worship involves dances in which special clothes and masks, like this one from Congo, are worn.

Strange trees called baobabs or 'bottle trees' grow on Madagascar. Their trunks store water in the dry months.

GABON

CONGO-BRAZZAVILLE

Congo

UGANDA

KENYA

Lake Victoria

RWANDA

NAIROBI

C O N G O

BURUNDI

Kasai

T A N Z A N I A

(Angola)

KINSHASA

DAR ES SALAAM

LUANDA

Lake Nyasa

LUBUMBASHI

MALAWI

ATLANTIC OCEAN

A N G O L A

Z A M B I A

M O Z A M B I Q U E

LUSAKA

Zambezi

HARARE

Namib Desert

ZIMBABWE

BOTSWANA

Limpopo

Kalahari Desert

MAPUTO

NAMIBIA

JOHANNESBURG

SWAZILAND

Orange

SOUTH AFRICA

LESOTHO

Cape of Good Hope

Scale

0   800 km

CAPE TOWN

The Maasai people come from East Africa, where they herd cattle. They wear the same beautiful ornaments that their ancestors did centuries ago. Girls older than nine adorn themselves with colourful necklaces and fantastic earrings.

Many countries of Southern Africa are rich in copper, diamonds, gold and other minerals. Miners drill the rock deep below the surface. Many local people are employed in the mines.

INDIAN
OCEAN

COMOROS

NTANANARIVO

ADAGASCAR

SOUTHERN AFRICA

T HE SOUTHERN half of Africa also has deserts: the Kalahari and the Namib in the southwest. But most of the region is covered either by rainforest, in the Congo Basin, or dry grasslands. The Great Rift Valley, a long 'crack' in the Earth's surface, runs down through East Africa, a region of mountains, volcanoes and long lakes.

Africa is famous for the huge variety of animals that roam across its plains. Giraffes, wildebeests, elephants, zebras and rhinoceroses live here, along with predators such as lions, cheetahs and hyenas.

DID YOU KNOW . . ?

Thousands of tourists visit Africa's wildlife parks, where the animals are protected by law. Unfortunately, many animals, such as elephants and rhinos, are killed by poachers, who then cut off and sell their tusks and horns. Some animals are now endangered.

Savannah, which is dry grassland with open woodland, covers the East African plains. Herds of animals, such as giraffes and zebras, live here.

WESTERN EUROPE

THE WESTERN lands of Europe stretch from the windy, wet Shetlands in the far north to the hot southern coasts of Spain and Portugal. The Atlantic Ocean brings cooling breezes in summer, but also mild weather in winter. The western coasts of the British Isles, Brittany and northwestern Spain have quite frequent rainfall. In the warmer, drier areas of France, Spain and Portugal, the climate is perfect for vineyards.

Shetland Is.

Amsterdam, capital of the Netherlands, is a city of fine old houses, canals and bridges.

NORTH SEA

NETHERLANDS
AMSTERDAM
BELGIUM
BRUSSELS
LUXEMBOURG
Meuse
PARIS
Seine
Loire
FRANCE
BRITTANY

ENGLISH CHANNEL

UNITED KINGDOM
SCOTLAND
GLASGOW
NORTHERN IRELAND
IRELAND
DUBLIN
ENGLAND
MANCHESTER
BIRMINGHAM
WALES
LONDON

The building of Stonehenge, England, was begun in about 3500 BC, 1000 years before the pyramids in Egypt. It may have been a place to observe the stars, or a temple of worship. The stones were quarried 300 km away.

The game of *pétanque* is very popular in France. It is played in most towns and villages. The object is to throw your ball as close as possible to a smaller ball.

ALPS

MONACO

Corsica

Rhône

MARSEILLE

MEDITERRANEAN SEA

BORDEAUX

BAY OF BISCAY

Garonne

ANDORRA

BARCELONA

P y r e n e e s

Ebro

BILBAO

Mallorca

VALENCIA

Balearic Islands

ATLANTIC OCEAN

Duero

S P A I N

MADRID

Tagus

Guadalquivir

SEVILLE

Gibraltar (Br.)

PORTO

P O R T U G A L

LISBON

Scale

0   300 km

The cathedral of La Sagrada Família (the Sacred Family) is one of the most amazing sights in Barcelona. Still unfinished today, it is a building of soaring towers and decorated stonework.

Forests of evergreen oak trees cover about one third of Portugal. The bark of these trees is used to make cork. It is stripped off and left to dry. Then it is steamed or boiled and pressed into sheets ready for use. The trees may provide cork bark for 100 years or more.

DID YOU KNOW . . ?

The United Kingdom, France, Netherlands, Spain and Portugal have all at one time possessed great overseas empires. In fact, nearly all of the Americas, Africa, Oceania and much of southern and southeast Asia have been ruled by one of these nations at some time in their history.

SOUTHERN EUROPE

THE LANDS of southern Europe border the Mediterranean and Black Seas. Italy and Greece are made up of peninsulas and islands. Rivers such as the Danube and its tributaries and the River Po in northern Italy flow across wide fertile plains, but most of southern Europe is hilly or mountainous.

The ancient Greek civilisation and the Roman Empire both began and spread across this region. Many historic remains still stand today.

The Parliament Building of Hungary stands on the eastern side of the River Danube in the capital, Budapest.

Building work began on the bell tower next to the Cathedral at Pisa, Italy, more than 800 years ago. Unfortunately, the ground beneath it was too soft and the tower began to lean. Today, engineers have made sure the Leaning Tower of Pisa will not fall over.

Marshes grow along the banks of the Danube near its mouth. Here, white pelicans come to nest in large numbers. They use their pouched bills to catch fish.

The ruins of buildings that were once magnificent temples are found all over Greece. This is Delphi, built on the slopes of Mount Parnassus. For the ancient Greeks, it was an important place of worship.

Scale
0   200 km

Southeast Europe is home to many different peoples and religions. This is a Muslim girl from Bosnia and Herzegovina.

DID YOU KNOW . . ?

The smallest country in the world is the Vatican City State. About one eighth the size of Central Park in New York, it lies inside Rome, capital of Italy. The Vatican is the home of the Pope. It has its own newspaper, bank and railway station.

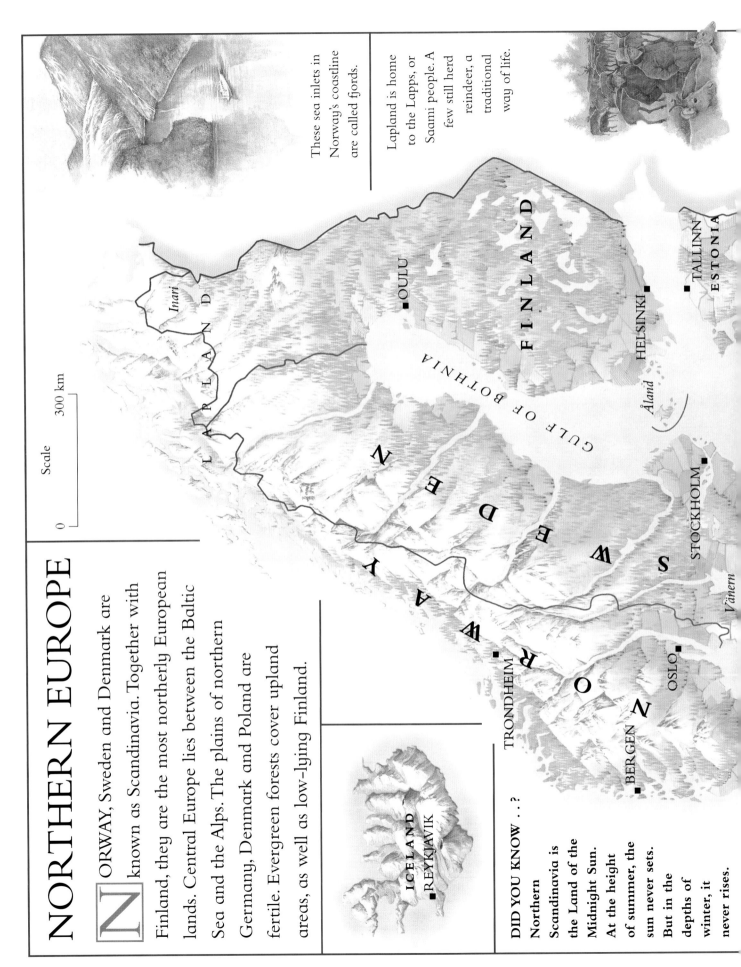

NORTHERN EUROPE

NORWAY, Sweden and Denmark are known as Scandinavia. Together with Finland, they are the most northerly European lands. Central Europe lies between the Baltic Sea and the Alps. The plains of northern Germany, Denmark and Poland are fertile. Evergreen forests cover upland areas, as well as low-lying Finland.

These sea inlets in Norway's coastline are called fjords.

Lapland is home to the Lapps, or Saami people. A few still herd reindeer, a traditional way of life.

Scale

0   300 km

DID YOU KNOW . . ?
Northern Scandinavia is the Land of the Midnight Sun. At the height of summer, the sun never sets. But in the depths of winter, it never rises.

ICELAND
■ REYKJAVIK

LAPLAND

Inari

■ OULU

FINLAND

TALLINN
■ ESTONIA

HELSINKI ■

Åland

GULF OF BOTHNIA

SWEDEN

STOCKHOLM ■

Vänern

NORWAY

TRONDHEIM ■

BERGEN ■

OSLO ■

Mountains cover much of Austria and Switzerland. Many Austrian village churches have onion-shaped domes.

The River Rhine in Germany is a major waterway. Barges carry goods up and down it. They pass through the Rhine gorge, a land of castles and vine-covered slopes.

This man shapes a blob of melted glass by blowing into it. Glassblowing is a traditional industry of Poland.

LATVIA

LITHUANIA

VILNIUS

(Russia)

BALTIC SEA

WARSAW

Vistula

P O L A N D

GDANSK

KRAKOW

SLOVAKIA

BRATISLAVA

DENMARK

COPENHAGEN

Bornholm

BERLIN

HAMBURG

Elbe

G E R M A N Y

PRAGUE

CZECH REPUBLIC

VIENNA

A U S T R I A

Danube

MUNICH

FRANKFURT

COLOGNE

Rhine

LIECHTENSTEIN

ZURICH

SWITZERLAND

A l p s

GENEVA

RUSSIA AND CENTRAL ASIA

RUSSIA is the largest country in the world. It stretches across two continents, Europe and Asia. Most of its people live in the European part, to the west of the Ural Mountains. Siberia, the Asian part, is a land of mountains and forests. It is bitterly cold for much of the year.

This train travels on the Trans-Siberian Railway, the longest railway in the world. A trip from Moscow to Vladivostok takes eight days.

DID YOU KNOW . . ?

Lake Baikal is the deepest lake in the world. From surface to bottom, it is four times the height of the tallest skyscraper.

L. Ladoga
ST. PETERSBURG
ARKHANGELSK
MINSK
BELARUS
MOSCOW
KIEV
MOLDOVA
UKRAINE
KHARKOV
ROSTOV
Volga
SAMARA
R U S S I A
Ural Mountains
YEKATERINBURG
Ob
Trans-Siberian Railway
OMSK
GEORGIA
Caspian Sea
KAZAKHSTAN
ARMENIA
AZER-BAIJAN
BAKU
Aral Sea
UZBEKISTAN
Lake Balkhash
TURKMENISTAN
SAMARKAND
KYRGYZSTAN
TAJIKISTAN
Novaya Zemlya

This colourful building is St. Basil's Cathedral in Moscow, the capital city of Russia.

Scale
0   800 km

ARCTIC
OCEAN

Lena

S I B E R I A

Tunguska

*Kamchatka
Peninsula*

SEA OF
OKHOTSK

Sakhalin

Amur

*Lake
Baikal*

IRKUTSK

VLADIVOSTOK

Besides Russians, about 100 different peoples live in Russia. This Nenets woman lives in the Arctic region of Siberia.

The Siberian crane is 1.5 metres tall. The male bird sometimes performs a kind of dance.

This is the great gateway of an ancient Islamic building in Samarkand, a city in Uzbekistan.

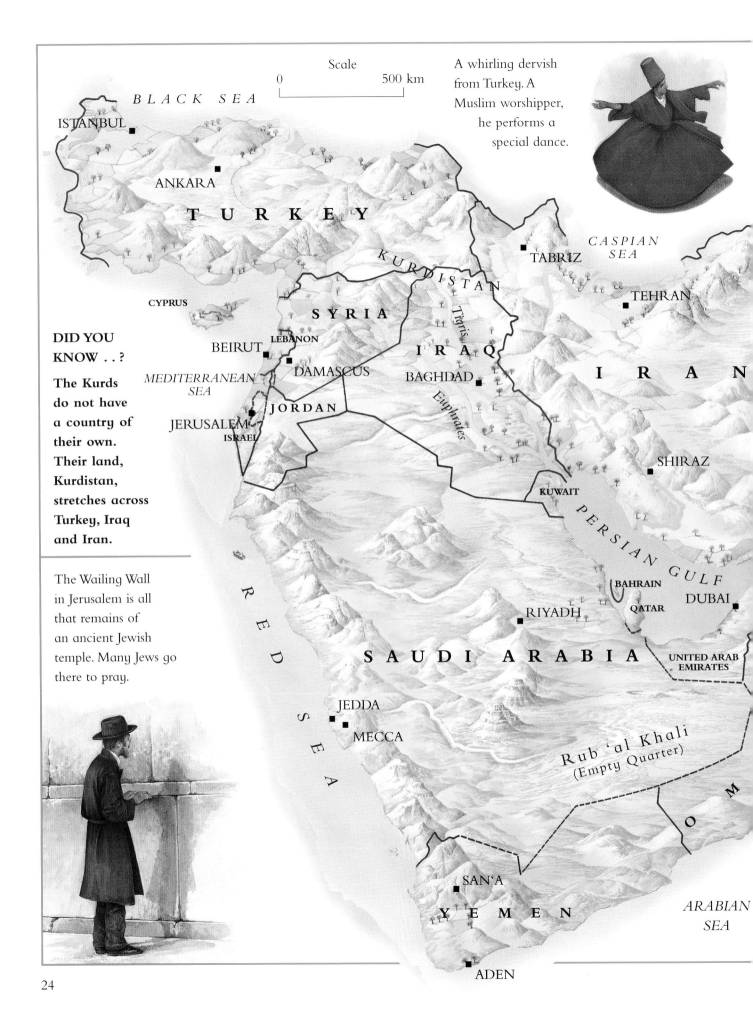

A whirling dervish from Turkey. A Muslim worshipper, he performs a special dance.

BLACK SEA

ISTANBUL

ANKARA

T U R K E Y

K U R D I S T A N

TABRIZ

CASPIAN SEA

CYPRUS

S Y R I A

TEHRAN

BEIRUT

LEBANON

Tigris

DID YOU KNOW . . ?

The Kurds do not have a country of their own. Their land, Kurdistan, stretches across Turkey, Iraq and Iran.

DAMASCUS

I R A Q

BAGHDAD

I R A N

MEDITERRANEAN SEA

JORDAN

Euphrates

JERUSALEM

ISRAEL

SHIRAZ

KUWAIT

P E R S I A N   G U L F

The Wailing Wall in Jerusalem is all that remains of an ancient Jewish temple. Many Jews go there to pray.

BAHRAIN

DUBAI

QATAR

RIYADH

R E D   S E A

S A U D I   A R A B I A

UNITED ARAB EMIRATES

JEDDA

MECCA

Rub 'al Khali (Empty Quarter)

O M

SAN'A

ARABIAN SEA

Y E M E N

ADEN

THE MIDDLE EAST

SOUTHWESTERN ASIA is also known as the Middle East. Much of this region is very dry, although parts of the Mediterranean coast and the area lying between the Tigris and Euphrates rivers in Iraq are richly fertile. The world's oldest farming settlements developed here. Turkey, Iran and Afghanistan are mountainous lands. Most of the Arabian Peninsula is desert.

MASHHAD

KABUL

AFGHANISTAN

MUSCAT

The Bedouin are nomads. They are a people who do not live in one place but wander with their animals across the desert lands of the Middle East.

The countries near the Persian Gulf have huge amounts of oil. It is transported to other countries around the world in tankers like this one.

The ancient city of San'a is the capital of Yemen. Lining its narrow, winding streets are these tall, carefully decorated houses. Built of stone and mud-brick with patterns made out of plaster, these early 'skyscrapers' are hundreds of years old.

Puppet shows are popular in Java, Indonesia. The puppets are carefully made out of flat card and moved by wires.

DID YOU KNOW . . ?

The world's tallest building, the Petronas Towers, is in Kuala Lumpur, Malaysia. It is 452 metres high.

Rice is the main crop of Southeast Asia. It is grown in waterlogged fields called paddies. In hilly areas, steps are built into the slopes so that the floodwaters do not flow away. This person is planting rice in paddies in Vietnam.

KASHMIR

LAHORE
PAKISTAN
Indus
KARACHI
Thar Desert
DELHI
NEPAL
H i m a l a y a s
BHUTAN
VARANASI
Ganges
BANGLADESH
DHAKA
I N D I A
KOLKATA (CALCUTTA)
BUR (MYAN
MUMBAI (BOMBAY)
Irrawaddy
BAY OF BENGAL
YANGO
CHENNAI (MADRAS)
Andam Islands (India)
SRI LANKA
COLOMBO
MALDIVES

For followers of the Hindu religion, the Ganges, like many of India's rivers, is a holy river. People have their ashes scattered in it after they die. Worshippers come to holy places, such as Varanasi, and bathe in the water.

'Giraffe-necked' women of Padaung, Burma, wear brass rings to make their necks grow longer.

INDIA AND SOUTHEAST ASIA

INDIA has the world's second highest population after China. Most of its people live in the countryside. India's best farmland is found in the plains of the River Ganges. To the north lie the Himalayas, the world's highest mountains. Across the Thar Desert in the east is Pakistan, another country with a large population.

Travelling east, we reach the tropical rainforests of Southeast Asia. In many parts, the trees are being felled to make way for farmland, cities, reservoirs or quarries.

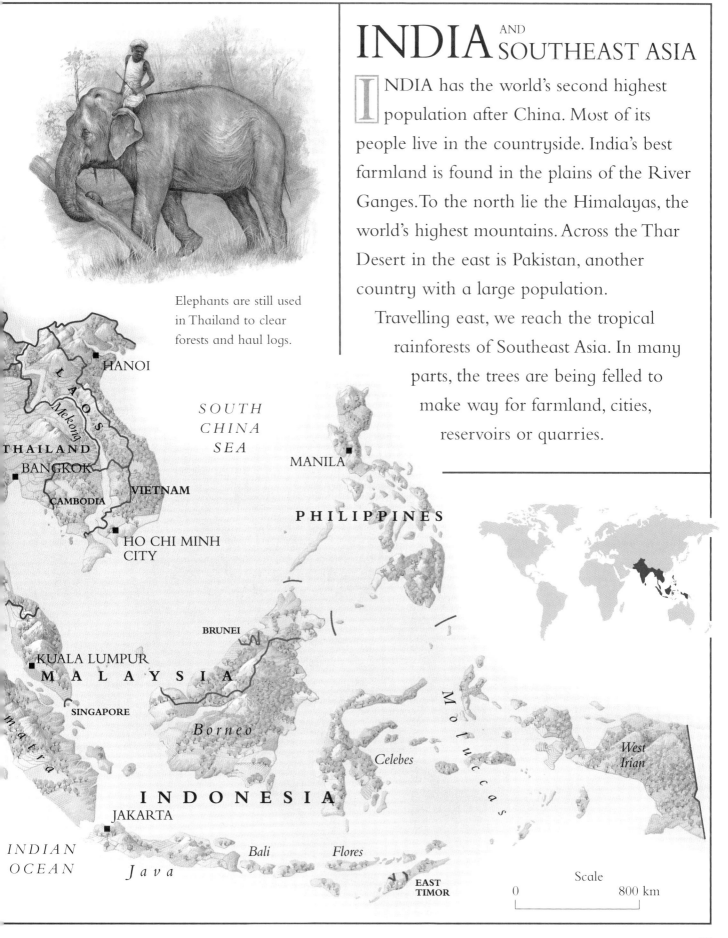

Elephants are still used in Thailand to clear forests and haul logs.

HANOI

LAOS

Mekong

THAILAND

BANGKOK

CAMBODIA

VIETNAM

HO CHI MINH CITY

SOUTH CHINA SEA

MANILA

PHILIPPINES

BRUNEI

KUALA LUMPUR

MALAYSIA

SINGAPORE

Borneo

Sumatra

INDONESIA

JAKARTA

INDIAN OCEAN

Java

Bali

Flores

Celebes

Moluccas

West Irian

EAST TIMOR

Scale

0   800 km

CHINA AND JAPAN

CHINA has the highest population of any country in the world. About a fifth of the world's people live there. The mountains and deserts of the west are mostly empty. Eastern China has rich farmland and great cities. Japan is made up of four main islands. Thousands of earthquakes happen there every year.

DID YOU KNOW . . ?

The main language of China is Mandarin. There are many spoken versions, but only one kind of writing, which everyone can understand.

On some Chinese rivers, fishermen train cormorants to catch fish for them.

Takla Makan

M O

G

C

Salween

Himalayas

The Great Wall of China was built to stop raiders from the north invading China. The Wall is more than 3000 kilometres long and is the largest structure ever built by people. It took many centuries to complete it.

In the Tibetan mountains, people live by herding yaks. This woman is churning yak's milk into butter.

Japan's capital, Tokyo, is one of the largest cities in the world. The underground trains are very crowded.

MANCHURIA

ULAN BATOR

HARBIN

OLIA

i

SEA OF JAPAN

SHENYANG

NORTH KOREA

BEIJING

PYONGYANG

JAPAN

TOKYO

TIANJIN

N   A

SEOUL

KYOTO

SOUTH KOREA

OSAKA

LANZHOU

Huang

Grand Canal

YELLOW SEA

KITAKYUSHU

XI'AN

NANJING

WUHAN

Yangtse

SHANGHAI

HANGZHOU

EAST CHINA SEA

Ryukyu Is.

CHONGQING

JIYANG

GUANGZHOU

HONG KONG

Scale

0   800 km

Hainan

Buddhism is one of the religions of Japan. A pagoda is a sacred place of Buddhist worship.

29

Many of Australia's amazing animals and birds are found nowhere else. This is a rainbow lorikeet.

Scale

0   500 km

INDIAN OCEAN

DARWIN

NORTHERN TERRITORY

Great Barrier Reef

QUEENSLAND

A U S T R A L I A

WESTERN AUSTRALIA

SOUTH AUSTRALIA

BRISBANE

Lake Eyre

Darling

NEW SOUTH WALES

PERTH

ADELAIDE

Murray

SYDNE

CANBERRA

VICTORIA

MELBOURNE

TASMANIA

A 'road train', a truck pulling several trailers, thunders across Australia's outback, alarming a group of kangaroos.

Sydney, Australia's largest city, is built around a natural harbour. Its most famous landmarks are the Harbour Bridge and the 'sail-roofed' Opera House.

Sheep farming is very important in both Australia and New Zealand. Together, they have more than 200 million sheep! Here, a shearer removes the fleece ~~of~~ a Merino sheep.

AUSTRALIA AND NEW ZEALAND

A USTRALIA and New Zealand are part of Oceania. This region also includes Papua New Guinea and the islands of the Pacific Ocean *(see pages 2-3)*.

Australia is large enough to be a continent itself. Nearly all its inhabitants live near the southeastern and south-western coasts. Here also are Australia's farmland and vineyards. The rest of the country is almost empty. Most of the western and central regions, known as the outback, are dry grassland or desert.

New Zealand is made up of two large mountainous islands. Its warm, rainy climate is perfect for farming.

DID YOU KNOW . . ?

The Great Barrier Reef, just off Australia's northeast coast, is the world's largest living thing. More than 2000 kilometres long, the reef is made of coral, the skeletons of tiny creatures. It is home to many kinds of fish.

AUCKLAND

North Island

TASMAN SEA

WELLINGTON

NEW ZEALAND

South Island

New Zealand was first inhabited by people only about 1000 years ago. The first settlers were the Maoris. They were fierce warriors. Today, people of Maori descent live in New Zealand's towns and cities. But they still keep alive the art, language and dances of their ancestors.

INDEX OF PLACE NAMES

HINKLER BOOKS

This edition first published in 2007
by Hinkler Books Pty Ltd
45–55 Fairchild St, Heatherton VIC 3202 Australia
www.hinklerbooks.com

© 2001 Orpheus Books Ltd.

Created and produced by Rachel Coombs, Nicholas Harris,
Sarah Harrison, Sarah Hartley and Emma Helbrough,
Orpheus Books Ltd.

Text: Anita Ganeri,
Prepress: Splitting Image
Cover design: Katy Wall

Illustrated by Susanna Addario, Graham Austin, Andrew Beckett,
John Butler, Martin Camm, Ferruccio Cucchiarini, Peter Dennis,
Malcolm Ellis, Betti Ferrero, Giuliano Fornari, Ray Grinaway, Gary
Hincks, Inklink, Ian Jackson, John Morris, Steve Noon, Eric Robson,
Nicki Palin, Claudia Saraceni, Ivan Stalio, Colin Woolf, David Wright

ISBN 978 1 7418 1279 4
10 9 8 7 6 5 4 3
10 12 11 09

Printed and bound in China